NANCY DREW

girl detective ®

CH

PAPERCUTZ

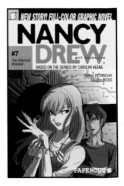

NANCY DREW

girl detective ®

#1

The Demon of River Heights

STEFAN PETRUCHA • Writer
SHO MURASE • Artist
with 3D CG elements by RACHEL ITO
Based on the series by
CAROLYN KEENE

New York

The Demon of River Heights
STEFAN PETRUCHA – Writer
SHO MURASE – Artist
with 3D CG elements by RACHEL ITO
BRYAN SENKA – Letterer
CARLOS JOSE GUZMAN
SHO MURASE
VAUGHN ROSS
Colorists
JIM SALICRUP
Editor-in-Chief

ISBN 10: 1-59707-000-9 paperback edition
ISBN 13: 978-1-59707-000-3 paperback edition
ISBN 10: 1-59707-004-1 hardcover edition
ISBN 13: 978-1-59707-004-1 hardcover edition

Printed in China.

10   9   8   7   6   5   4

BESS IS DURABLE, ONE OF THE BRAVEST PEOPLE I KNOW, BUT I THINK THE DEMON-TALK FROM THE MOVIE PUT US ALL A LITTLE ON EDGE.

AS FOR ME, I KNOW RIVER HEIGHTS HAS PLENTY OF WILDLIFE, DEER, CHIPMUNKS, THE INCREDIBLY *RARE* BEAR, AND, FOR SOME REASON, MORE THAN ITS SHARE OF *CRIME!*

BUT SO FAR... *NO* MONSTERS!

OKAY, SEARCH TEAM, GRAB YOUR FLASH-LIGHTS AND CELL PHONES, AND LET'S SEE WHAT WE CAN SEE!

IT TURNED OUT WE COULDN'T SEE *MUCH*. THE WOODS GET PITCH *BLACK* ON MOONLESS NIGHTS LIKE THIS.

GEORGE WAS ABSOLUTELY *RIGHT* ABOUT MY TIMING...

BUT I COULDN'T HELP NOTICING THAT A STRANGE *FIGURE* HAD COME UPON BEN AND QUENTIN...

Replay

Replay

AND *THAT* WAS WHEN THEY DROPPED THEIR EQUIPMENT.

WHAT WAS IT? PART OF THEIR FILM? I DON'T BELIEVE IN *MONSTERS*.

NOT *USUALLY*.

AS I SAID, SOMETIMES I JUST GET SO *WRAPPED UP* IN A CASE, I FORGET *EVERYTHING* ELSE.

IMPORTANT THINGS, TOO, THINGS LIKE...

FOR INSTANCE, I'VE BEEN CARRYING AROUND THIS UNLIT CIGARETTE FOR THE TEN YEARS SINCE I QUIT.

MY DOCTORS INSIST IT'S UNWISE TO KEEP TEMPTATION SO CLOSE AT HAND, BUT I BELIEVE IT MAKES ME *STRONGER.*

AFTER ALL, IF YOUR *MONSTER* COULD BE *REAL,* WHAT COULDN'T?

SO I'M NOT PREPARED TO ACCEPT WHAT *OTHER* PEOPLE TAKE FOR FACT.

BUT LET'S JUST SAY I DON'T NECESSARILY *BELIEVE* WHAT *EVERYONE* KNOWS.

I'D RATHER *NOT* DISCUSS THAT, ESPECIALLY SINCE I'M NO LONGER USING YOUR *FATHER* AS MY ATTORNEY.

SO, MR. ANGLEY, WHAT SORT OF BUSINESS ARE YOU GOING TO OPEN IN RIVER HEIGHTS?

ARE YOU GETTING OUT OF MINING? I MEAN, EVERYONE KNOWS ALL THE ORE'S TAPPED OUT AROUND HERE.

BUT THAT DIDN'T MAKE ME ANY *LESS* SUSPICIOUS OF OUR "RESCUER."

I'M HERE PRETTY OFTEN MYSELF, VISITING NED, OR JUST USING THE LIBRARY, SO I KNEW MY WAY AROUND.

WILDER U IS WHERE NED STUDIES ENGLISH, BUT IT'S A BIG ENOUGH PLACE TO OFFER EVERYTHING FROM FILM STUDIES TO PRE-MED.

COMFORTABLE THAT THINGS WERE WELL IN HAND BACK HOME, I MADE THE DRIVE IN A FEW HOURS.

OF COURSE, I'D
PROBABLY KEEP
MY DOOR LOCKED.

I ALWAYS WONDERED WHAT
IT WOULD BE LIKE LIVING IN A
DORM. I HAD ALL THE FREEDOM
I NEEDED AT HOME, BUT IT
STILL LOOKED KIND OF FUN.

THEN AGAIN, I
PROBABLY COULD
HAVE PICKED IT OUT
WITHOUT ANY HELP!
HE SURE SEEMED
A TIRELESS SELF-
PROMOTER!

IT WAS EASY ENOUGH TO FIND
QUENTIN'S DORM ROOM LISTED
IN THE STUDENT DIRECTORY.

I WASN'T SURE WHAT TO BELIEVE. MAYBE BEN AND QUENTIN WERE OUT THERE SAFELY CAMPED IN THE WOODS, *LAUGHING* AT US.

MAYBE THEY JUST *CHANGED* THEIR COSTUME AT THE LAST MINUTE. OR MAYBE *NOT*.

I WANTED TO GO BACK TO THE WOODS, LOOK FOR MORE CLUES. BUT IT WAS GETTING LATE. TIME TO GET HOME.

OHHHH! OUT OF GAS *AGAIN*!

BESS IS GOING TO *KILL* ME! HECK, IF I WEREN'T ME, *I'D* KILL ME!

WRRR....
WRRR....
WRR...

OH WELL, NOT TOO LATE TO CALL MY AAA PAL, CHARLES ADAMS. HE SAYS HE KEEPS A CAN OF GAS BY HIS TRUCK WITH MY NAME ON IT!

CHARLIE? CAN YOU HEAR ME? I'M STUCK BY FOREST ROAD, NEAR THE...

NRGHTHY -CLICK- NANCY? PHSGHHRLLLL?

BUT IT WASN'T THEM, AND THIS WAS NO MOVIE SET.

THERE WERE LOTS OF OLD IRON MINES IN THE WOODS SURROUNDING RIVER HEIGHTS.

I'D BEEN IN A FEW. THEY WERE RICKETY AND DANGEROUS, SO I'D CERTAINLY NEVER GO BACK INSIDE ONE UNLESS I HAD TO.

BUT, THE THING IS, THEY WERE ALL *ABANDONED*.

THIS ONE, CLEARLY, WAS *NOT*.

BEFORE THEY CAUGHT UP.

BUT ONLY FOR A SECOND.

THAT WAS HOW I FELT WHEN I SAW MY CAR.

AND THEN, WELL... EVER HAVE THAT TERRIFIC MOMENT OF *RELIEF*, LIKE AT THE END OF A RACE WHEN YOU REALIZE YOU'VE *WON*?

I RAN, FAST AS I COULD, BRANCHES SCRATCHING MY ARMS AND LEGS, TERRIFIED I WOULD FALL.

LAST TIME, THERE WAS ONE MONSTER TO THREE GIRLS, NOW THE ODDS WERE *REVERSED.*

UMF!

THIS WAY, I'D FINALLY GET TO THE BOTTOM OF THINGS.

I COULD HAVE STRUGGLED MORE, BUT IF I RAN AWAY, I'D BE BACK AT SQUARE ONE.

THIS ONE HAD ME BY MY ARMS!

USUALLY, A MYSTERY DRAGS ME AROUND BY THE NOSE.

UH-OH.

C-CRACCKKK

WHUNK

UNGH!

WHAP

DON'T YOU KNOW WHEN TO QUIT? THIS AIN'T NO MOVIE!

GET AWAY FROM HER!

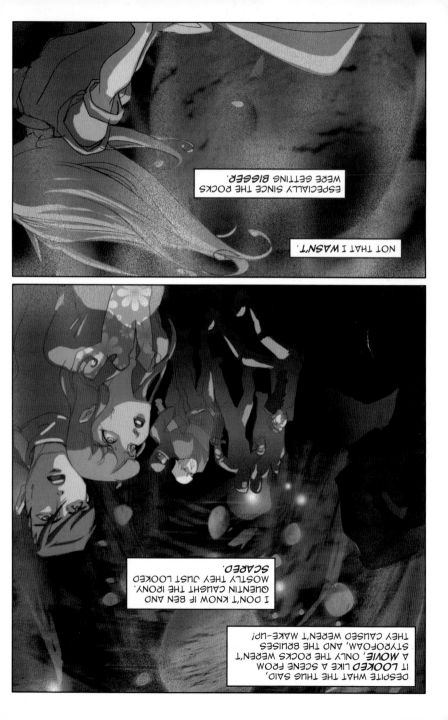

NOT THAT I WASN'T.

ESPECIALLY SINCE THE ROCKS WERE GETTING BIGGER.

I DON'T KNOW IF BEN AND QUENTIN CAUGHT THE IRONY. MOSTLY THEY JUST LOOKED SCARED.

DESPITE WHAT THE THUG SAID, IT LOOKED LIKE A SCENE FROM A MOVIE, ONLY THE ROCKS WEREN'T STYROFOAM, AND THE BRUISES THEY CAUSED WEREN'T WAKE-UP!

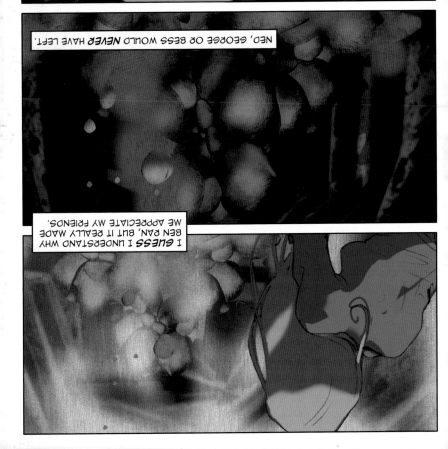

I CERTAINLY WISHED *THEY* WERE HERE! NO WAY COULD I DIG OUT BY MYSELF, AND I CERTAINLY WASN'T GOING TO DRAG CANTON ANGLEY AROUND BY MYSELF *AND* FIND ANOTHER EXIT.

NED, GEORGE OR BESS WOULD *NEVER* HAVE LEFT.

I *GUESS* I UNDERSTAND WHY BEN RAN, BUT IT REALLY MADE ME APPRECIATE MY FRIENDS.

SOME OF THESE COULD BE HUNDREDS OF YARDS *DEEP!*

THE OLD *ELEVATOR SHAFTS* WERE USUALLY DUG NEAR THE VENTILATION. A FACT I REMEMBERED A LITTLE TOO *LATE.*

ESPECIALLY SINCE THIS TIME, I KNEW WHO IT WAS.

SO *ONE* MORE DIDN'T MAKE MUCH OF A DIFFERENCE.

ASIDE FROM DANGLING, I WAS ACTUALLY GETTING USED TO ALL THE *SHADOWY FIGURES* I'D BEEN SEEING LATELY.

WATCH OUT FOR PAPERCUTZ™
The publisher of graphic novels created just for YOU!

Find out more about the big brains behind Papercutz on page 98.

TOTALLY SPIES! is now a part of the Papercutz line of super-stars! Discover new secrets about your favorite secret agents on page 100.

Papercutz is also proud to present a special graphic novel, THE LIFE OF POPE JOHN PAUL II ...*IN COMICS*! For more details about this major event in graphic novel publishing proceed to page 103.

There's big news in store for NANCY DREW, GIRL DETECTIVE! The star of the best-selling series of Papercutz graphic novels is heading for Hollywood! We've got the inside story starting on page 105.

THE HARDY BOYS have been on a wild and crazy ride since their very first Papercutz graphic novel. Check out where they've been and where they're going on page 108.

Fans have suggested that the "Z" in Papercutz stands for ZORRO! See for yourself the amazing cast of characters Zorro has encountered in his series of Papercutz graphic novels starting on page 111.

PAPERCUT**Z**™

This is the amazing tale of two men, born days apart, who have devoted their lives to comics. Terry Nantier, is a pioneer in the world of graphic novels, who for over thirty years has published work by the greatest artists and writers in the world – Will Eisner, Milton Caniff, P. Craig Russell, Lewis Trondheim, and many more. His partner in this new project, Jim Salicrup, started in comics when he was a wee lad of fifteen years old, and went on to become one of the most successful editors in the field, editing top titles such as the X-Men, the X-Files, the Fantastic Four, Dracula, and many more, including Spider-Man # 1 – the best-selling Spider-Man comic of all time.

A few years ago, Terry observed that most comics publishers were ignoring a vast potential audience of tweens and teens and focusing too much on older long-time comics fans. Seeing this opportunity to create a new generation of graphic novels for a new generation of fans, Terry and Jim went to work at once to make their vision a reality. The plan was simple— cool characters, in great stories, published in full-color in a digest-sized format. The best parts of traditional American comics would be combined with the most exciting elements of Japanese comics (called manga).

But what should they call this new comics company? Sylvia Nantier, Terry's brilliant daughter, suggested the name, and *Papercutz* was born.

In 2005 the debut Papercutz graphic novels were published – NANCY DREW, GIRL DETECTIVE and THE HARDY BOYS, with new books following every three months. And right from the start, fans loved the Papercutz approach — the first NANCY DREW, GIRL DETECTIVE graphic novel went into three big printings in its first year!

To stay on top of everything that's coming your way from Papercutz, we've created this special bonus feature. Everything you see presented in these pages is available now at your favorite booksellers. To get even more up-to-date news, be sure to visit www.papercutz.com.

Terry and Jim want to thank each and every one of you for picking up this Papercutz graphic novel. Don't be shy— let us know what you think. After all, we're working hard to produce stories that are not only fun and entertaining – but also respect your intelligence. Send your comments to our Editor-in-Chief: salicrup@papercutz.com

Caricatures by Steve Brodner.

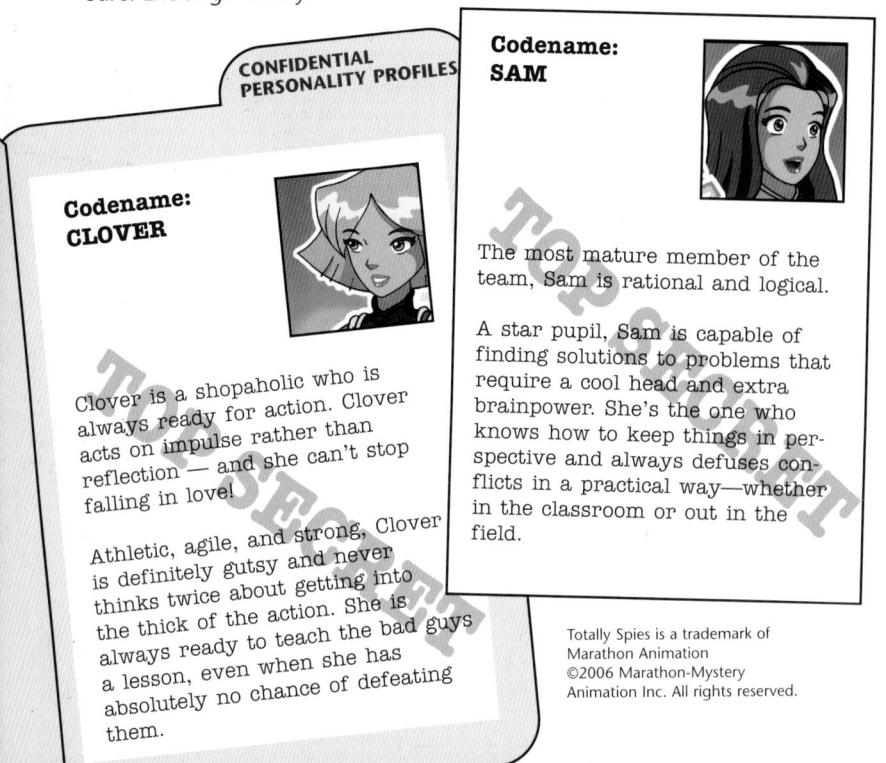

They're here! TV's sensational secret agents on Cartoon Network are now starring in their own series of full-color graphic novels from Papercutz! Each Totally Spies! graphic novel features two big adventures starring Clover, Sam, and Alex doing what they do best—having fun while foiling the schemes of the wildest and wackiest criminal masterminds!

Sam, Alex, and Clover are three High School girls who fight crime on an international scale as undercover agents for the World Organization of Human Protection – WOOHP! Stressful? Sure. Exciting? Totally.

CONFIDENTIAL
PERSONALITY PROFILES

**Codename:
CLOVER**

Clover is a shopaholic who is always ready for action. Clover acts on impulse rather than reflection — and she can't stop falling in love!

Athletic, agile, and strong, Clover is definitely gutsy and never thinks twice about getting into the thick of the action. She is always ready to teach the bad guys a lesson, even when she has absolutely no chance of defeating them.

**Codename:
SAM**

The most mature member of the team, Sam is rational and logical.

A star pupil, Sam is capable of finding solutions to problems that require a cool head and extra brainpower. She's the one who knows how to keep things in perspective and always defuses conflicts in a practical way—whether in the classroom or out in the field.

Codename:
ALEX

Alex, the youngest member of the team, is also the most affectionate. She admires her older friends, Sam and Clover, enormously and is determined to place their relationships above all else.

Being the youngest, Alex is also a bit gullible. She's frequently fooled by the baddies... as well as by her friends! Fortunately, Alex is very good-natured and never turns it into a big deal.

Codename:
MANDY

Mandy is Alex, Sam, and Clover's worst nightmare. She is in the same class as our three heroines. Overly self-assured, pretentious, and opinionated, Mandy is a real pest. Whether she's trying to get involved with the girls' private lives or desperately trying to outdo them in order to look cool, Mandy is always around the corner just waiting to cause the girls trouble.

Codename:
JERRY

As the head of the international secret agent organization WOOPH, Jerry thinks nothing of whisking the girls away from their daily lives to send them off in hot pursuit of a crazy villain halfway around the world!

Both a mentor and an instructor, Jerry is a second father to the girls. He's always there to congratulate them at the end of a successful mission.

RIDES OF THE PAPERCUTZ STARS

The souped-up **NPU 3000** is the ultimate spy car – or is it? Find out in Totally Spies! #1!

JOHN PAUL II
...IN COMICS!

This special Papercutz graphic novel tells the dramatic story of Karol Wojtyla's life, from his boyhood in Poland to his sad final hours in the Vatican. It's the inspirational story of a man who loved humanity and devoted his life to his beliefs. As His Eminence Cardinal Jose Saraiva Martins, prefect of the Congregation for Saints' Causes writes in his introduction, the Pope's "message was undoubtedly understood foremost by the young to whom (this graphic novel is) ...primarily dedicated." Originally published in Italy, it's written by Alessandro Mainardi and illustrated by Werner Maresta.

Born May 18, 1920, Karol Jozef Wojtyla reigned as pope of the Roman Catholic Church from 1978 until his death, almost 27 years later. He was the first non-Italian pope since the 16th century and the only Polish pope ever. In his early years as pope, he was known for speaking out against Communism, and considered one of the factors that helped bring about its fall.

Even in his final years he was unafraid to speak out, and criticized contemporary greed in the forms of consumerism and out-of-control capitalism.

During his reign, the pope visited over 100 countries, more than any previous pope. While he was Pope the influence of the Church expanded in the Third World.

Pope John Paul II was well-loved worldwide, attracting the largest crowds in history. Attracting crowds of over one million people in a single venue and over four million people at the World Youth Day in Manila.

On April 2, 2005, at 9:37 PM local time, Pope John Paul II died after struggling with Parkinson's Disease, amongst other diseases, for many years. Millions of people flocked to Rome to pay their respects to the body and for his funeral.

This special Papercutz graphic novel is published at the larger 6" x 9" size, in full-color, as a jacketed hardcover, available at booksellers everywhere.

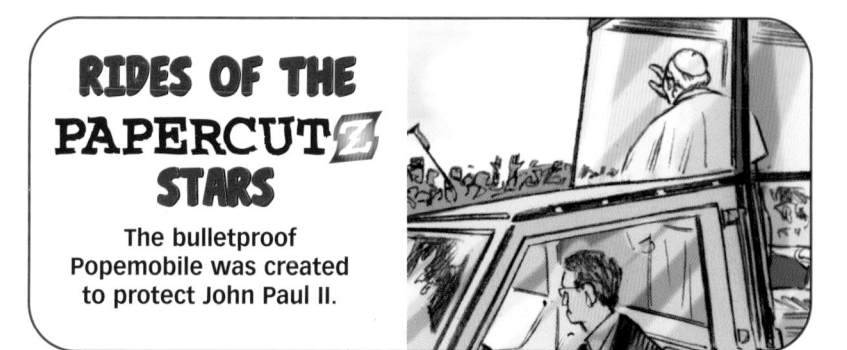

RIDES OF THE PAPERCUTZ STARS

The bulletproof Popemobile was created to protect John Paul II.

NANCY DREW
GOES HOLLYWOOD!

Production commenced in Los Angeles on the live-action mystery adventure movie *Nancy Drew*, starring Emma Roberts (Nickelodeon's *Unfabulous*), Josh Flitter (*The Greatest Game Ever Played*), Max Thieriot (*The Pacifier*) and Tate Donovan (*Good Night, and Good Luck, The O.C.*) as Nancy's dad, Carson Drew. The movie is directed by Andrew Fleming.

In a published interview, Emma has revealed that she's "rather nervous because so many generations have read the books and I have big shoes to fill. But I'm really excited and it's going to be a lot of fun"

Nancy Drew is set to appear at the theater near you in August 2007, from Warner Bros. Pictures, a Warner Bros. Entertainment Company.

NANCY DREW Graphic Novel Episode Guide

Here's a great way to keep track of the Papercutz
Nancy Drew, Girl Detective graphic novels…

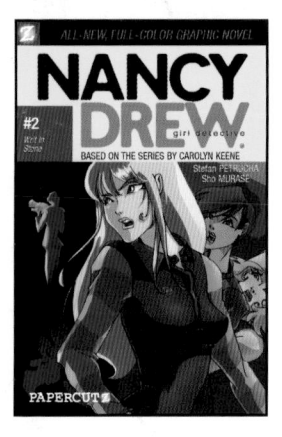

Nancy Drew graphic novel #1

"The Demon of River Heights"
Stefan Petrucha, writer, and Sho Murase, artist
Join Nancy, along with Bess and George, as
they search for missing student filmmakers
and discover the deadly secret behind the
local urban legend known as "The Demon
of River Heights."

Nancy Drew graphic novel #2

"Writ In Stone"
Stefan Petrucha, writer, and Sho Murase, artist
It's double trouble for Nancy and her
friends, when an ancient artifact and a little
boy are both suddenly missing. Nancy's
determined to recover both the artifact and
little Owen, but someone's out to stop her
– *permanently!*

Nancy Drew graphic novel #3

"The Haunted Dollhouse"
Stefan Petrucha, writer, and Sho Murase, artist
River Heights is celebrating "Nostalgia
Week," and everyone in town is dressing up
like it's 1930. But the fun is soon interrupt-
ed when the dolls in Emma Blavatsky's
antique dollhouse seem to come alive and
start depicting strange crimes that soon
come true in real life. When Nancy stakes
out the dollhouse, she witnesses a doll ver-
sion of herself murdered!

Nancy Drew graphic novel #4

"The Girl Who Wasn't There"
Stefan Petrucha, writer, and Sho Murase, artist
Nancy receives a desperate call for help from Kalpana, her new friend in India. Soon, Nancy, along with Bess and George, are in New Delhi, looking for Kalpana, where not even Sahadev, a powerful crime lord, can scare Nancy off the case!

Nancy Drew graphic novel #5

"The Fake Heir"
Stefan Petrucha, writer, and Vaughn Ross, artist
Nancy Drew may have lost her ability to solve a mystery! It's totally embarrassing for Nancy to confront the very much alive Mr. Druthers — the man she claimed was murdered by his wife.

RIDES OF THE PAPERCUTZ STARS

Normally, Nancy Drew drives her gasoline-electric hybrid car, but she drove this roadster during Nostalgia Week.

THE HARDY BOYS ®

Sam, Clover, and Alex, agents of WOOHP (World Organization of Human Protection), who are now battling the forces of LAMOS (League Aiming to Menace and Overthrow Spies), aren't the only spies lurking within the pages of Papercutz graphic novels! There was this guy, who Frank and Joe Hardy rescued in Hardy Boys graphic novel # 3...

The Hardy Boys ® Simon & Schuster

And, of course, Frank and Joe Hardy are now themselves under-cover brothers working for ATAC (American Teens Against Crime), the secret organization created by their dad, Fenton Hardy.

Recently, Papercutz Editor-in-Chief, Jim Salicrup had the pleasure of meeting Robert Vaughn, who played TV super-spy, Napoleon Solo on the classic The Man From U.N.C.L.E. (United Network Command for Law and Enforce-ment). Here the Man From Uncle checks out Hardy Boys graphic novel # 1, as The Man From MoCCA (Museum of Comic and Cartoon Art) looks on...

THE HARDY BOYS Graphic Novel Episode Guide

America's favorite undercover brothers star in an all-new, full-color series of Papercutz graphic novels, with all-new comics stories based on the series by Franklin W. Dixon.

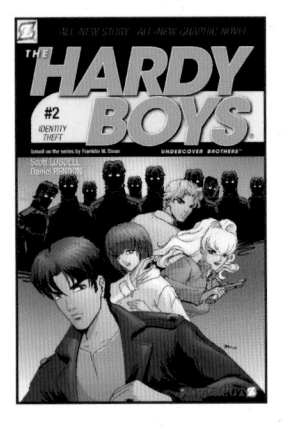

The Hardy Boys graphic novel #1

"The Ocean of Osyria"

Scott Lobdell, writer, and Lea Hernandez, artist

Frank and Joe Hardy, with Callie and Iola, search for a missing Mid-Eastern art treasure — "The Ocean of Osyria" — to free their friend, Chet Morton, who has been falsely accused of stealing it! It's like a blockbuster movie in comics form featuring your favorite teen sleuths!

The Hardy Boys graphic novel #2

"Identity Theft"

Scott Lobdell, writer, Daniel Rendon, artist

Frank and Joe Hardy, are assigned a fantastic case of stolen identity — literally! Joy Gallagher claims another girl is now living her life, with her parents, and in her body! Is she insane? Or can her story actually be true? Featuring a special guest-appearance by Mr. Snuggles!

The Hardy Boys graphic novel #3

"Mad House"

Scott Lobdell, writer, Daniel Rendon, artist

Frank and Joe Hardy go undercover on the hit reality TV series "Mad House," the show in which contestants must live together in a house while cameras record their every move, to solve the mystery of who is harming the contestants— and why?! But things go from bad to worse when the Hardy Boys stumble upon a shocking murder!

The Hardy Boys graphic novel #4

"Malled"

Scott Lobdell, writer, Daniel Rendon, artist

Bayport's much-publicized new mall is about to open, but when suspicious accidents keep happening, ATAC sends Frank and Joe Hardy to investigate! The night before the Mall's Grand Opening, Frank, Joe, and eight others are mysteriously locked in the mall— with a murderer on the loose!

The Hardy Boys graphic novel #5

"Sea You, Sea Me"

Scott Lobdell, writer, Daniel Rendon, artist

The Hardy Boys get caught in a perfect storm! Frank and Joe go undercover aboard "the Silver Lining," an old fishing boat, to find out why teen crew members keep mysteriously vanishing. The number of suspects dwindles when one of the crew turns up dead!

RIDES OF THE PAPERCUTZ STARS

Frank and Joe prefer motorcycles to cars.

ZORRO

The Papercutz Zorro graphic novels are unlike any other Zorro comics ever published before. The obvious difference is the Japanese comics style look of Sidney Lima's artwork. But the really big difference is that Zorro's new adventures take place outside of the pueblo de Los Angeles. Why would that community's legendary hero ever leave? The answer to that question is this woman:

Eulalia, risked her life to save Zorro from being shot by Commandante Monasterio. Enraged, he struck her across her face with his gun, scarring her, and sentenced her to death. Fortunately, Zorro has returned the favor, and rescued her before she could be executed. Now Zorro and Eulalia are on the run from Monasterio, who is determined to kill them both!

Zorro graphic novel #1

"Scars!"

Don McGregor, writer and Sidney Lima, artist

Zorro and Eulalia wind up in literally uncharted territory, and actually meet a mapmaker and his wife who are on the run from Lucifer Trapp, a man determined to keep this territory undiscovered at any cost!

Zorro graphic novel #2

Don McGregor, writer and Sidney Lima, artist

"Drownings!" takes Zorro and Eulaia even farther away from Los Angeles, as they run into a couple fleeing the deadly Scorched Brothers. But after being with Eulalia day and night for several weeks, can Zorro seriously hope to keep his identity secret from Eulalia? What happens when Zorro is finally unmasked?

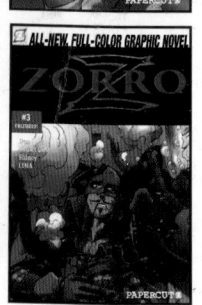

Zorro graphic novel #3

Don McGregor, writer and Sidney Lima, artist

"Vultures!" proves that wherever Zorro and Eulalia go, they are sure to encounter trouble! Zorro must save Normandie Caniff from becoming the next victim of a con artist called Lockspur. That's not easy to do when you're tied to stakes and being served up as dinner for ravenous vultures!

Will Zorro ever find a safe haven for the woman who saved his life? Or are they destined to be on the run forever?

RIDES OF THE PAPERCUTZ STARS

More than a means of transportation, the great black stallion, Tornado, is Zorro's friend.